MW00895955

EXTREME SURVIVORS

BLACKBIRCH PRESS

An imprint of Thomson Gale, a part of The Thomson Corporation

THOMSON

GALE

Detroit • New York • San Francisco • San Diego • New Haven, Conn. • Waterville, Maine • London • Munich

THOMSON
★
GALE

Photo credits: cover: Photos.com, Corel Corporation; all pages © Discovery Communications, Inc. except for pages 4, 8, 12, 16, 24, 28, 32, 33 © Corel Corporation; page 20 © Photos.com; page 36 © Lonely Planet; page 40 © Photo Researchers

LIBRARY OF CONGRESS CATALOGING-IN-PUBLICATION DATA

Survivors / Marla Felkins Ryan, book editor
  p. cm. — (Planet's most extreme)

Includes bibliographical references and index.
  ISBN: 1-4103-0382-9 (hard cover : alk. paper)
    1-4103-0340-3 (paper cover : alk. paper)
  1. Animal behavior—Juvenile literature. 2. Risk-taking (Psychology) — Juvenile litera-ture. I. Ryan, Marla Felkins, 1958- II. Title III. Series.

Printed in the United States of America
10 9 8 7 6 5 4 3 2 1

Are you a survivor? Could you hang tough with animals living in the worst conditions on the planet? We're counting down the top ten most extreme survivors in the animal kingdom and seeing how humans stack up against their extraordinary endurance. Discover that when the going gets tough, the tough get pushed to The Most Extreme.

10

The Camel

Our countdown begins in a land of extremes—extreme heat, and extreme dryness. You have to be tough to survive in a desert. That's why camels come in at number ten in our countdown. For thousands of years, people have been crossing the arid wastelands of Arabia on these animals known as "ships of the desert."

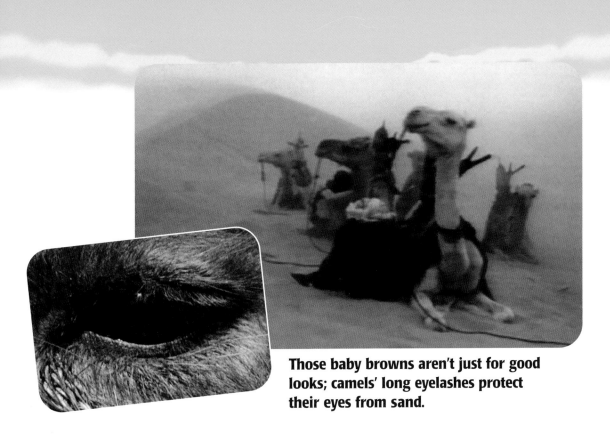

Those baby browns aren't just for good looks; camels' long eyelashes protect their eyes from sand.

Other people have been less complimentary and called them "horses designed by committee." But the committee knew what it was doing. The camel might be ugly, but it survives in conditions that no horse ever could, as camel breeder Gil Reigler explains:

> Camels have amazing adaptation to the desert. It's arid, it's hot, and there's not much food. But look how big these animals grow and how strong they are. They can carry 600 pounds of weight for ten hours a day, without that much water or food. Everything about them is adapted to their environment. Their nostrils are little slits and they have special muscles that close them during a sandstorm. The little hairs inside will siphon out the sand so they can actually breathe. Long eyelashes keep the sand away from the eyes. And they also have a second eyelid that goes across it, so they can walk in the desert with this eyelid covering the eye.

A little fat in the hump is a good thing when it can keep you alive in the desert for days.

The camel's most famous feature also comes in handy in the desert. But contrary to popular opinion, its hump doesn't store water. It's actually full of fat, which the camel can use as a fuel supply in times of adversity.

So with all these built-in survival features, just how tough is a camel?

Imagine you are dropped into a desert. There's no water and no shade, and the temperature is 120 degrees. In this extreme heat you start sweating at an alarming rate. Sweating drains your body fluids. Lose more than 12 percent of your body weight and you're in big trouble. With nothing to drink, you'll be dead in less than 36 hours.

Now imagine you had the super-survival skills of the camel. You'd be able to endure the extreme heat much longer. That's because not only is the camel better at conserving water, it can also lose more than 25 percent of its body weight and still survive. It can go without a drink for an incredible 8 days! So when it finally finds water, no wonder it can drink 21 gallons—in 10 minutes!

It's a different kind of drinking that may take the camel out of the desert and into our homes. Gil Reigler explains:

Camel milk is very nutritious. When you think about the desert there really isn't anything there. Especially when you think about fruits or vegetables than can supply vitamin C for the young baby camels. Camel milk contains triple the amount of vitamin C that cow's milk contains. It also contains insulin, and we're very interested in doing the research to find out how this insulin works with diabetics.

Gil has set up the first camel dairy in the United States. It's not a new idea. In deserts around the world, many people rely on this nutritious milk for survival. And Gil has discovered that camel milk has 40 percent less choles- terol than cow's milk, and will keep for 4 months in the fridge. It's a long way from the deserts of Arabia to the fridges of America, but who knows . . . maybe one day we'll be calling the camel the "cow of the desert."

Got camel milk? Gil Reigler says it contains three times the vitamin C of cow's milk.

9

The **Rat**

Welcome to Drybones, Texas. It's time for a showdown with pest controller Michael Bohdan. Number nine in our countdown is also public enemy number one. It's the rat.

Bohdan explains:

Rats have been around for millions of years, and they've always associated themselves with man, and as a result they've been able to adapt their life and they're very prolific. It doesn't take very long for a rodent to be born and then let's say 30 or 45 days later it starts having young of it's own.

Imagine being a rat and having your own rat babies before you were 2 months old!

At this rate a single pair of rats could have fifteen thousand offspring in a year—if they all survived. And surviving is what rats do best.

Rats are number nine in our countdown because they're so tough. They have to be, because we try really hard to get rid of them (and the diseases they carry). But rats just keep coming back for more. Take a look at most cities and you'll find for every person there's at least one rat making itself at home.

So how do these wily rodents always stay one jump ahead of us? For a start, rats are incredible athletes. Their superhuman powers mean they can come into our lives through even the most unlikely entrances. Have you ever dreamed of what it would be like to have the super powers of a rat?

Not even a super-rat, this guy can gnaw through lead pipes and cinderblocks.

If you were a rat, you'd be able to squeeze into some very small spaces! Thanks to flexible bones in your skull, you'd be able to squeeze through any hole that's just slightly bigger than the width of your head! And you'd never get stuck in a pipe because the jaws of a rat are 120 times stronger than human ones! That means you could easily gnaw a hole in a lead pipe, or a garbage can, or even cinderblocks!

And because rats are so much smaller and lighter than humans, they have no trouble falling great distances. With the super powers of a rat you could survive a fall from a 5-story building! That's why we've had to try every trick in the book to get rid of these super survivors.

Poisons are our favorite anti-rat weapon, but rats have even found ways to survive chemical warfare. It seems rats take tiny bites of any new food they find, including poisons, which may help them build up an immunity. Coupled with the rat's fast reproductive rate, this has seen the emergence of super-rats–animals that scientists have described as "little bags of poison with four legs and a tail."

One man shared the rat's incredible tolerance of poison. He was the scandalous mad monk Rasputin. By 1916 in Tsarist Russia, Rasputin had become so unpopular that a band of conspirators decided to poison him with food laced with cyanide.

Rats have built up immunities to even the most extreme man-made poisons.

But he didn't die. The poison may not have worked because Rasputin's chronic gastritis meant the cyanide wasn't rendered volatile. So like a rat, Rasputin cheated death. Until the conspirators decided to shoot him . . . several times.

And still he didn't die. It wasn't until they beat him about the head and threw him in the river that Rasputin finally succumbed. But not to the poison, or the bullets, but by drowning.

8

The Gannet

Even though rats are harder to kill than Rasputin, they're still only number nine in our most extreme countdown. At number eight is an animal so tough it doesn't need health insurance … because it can walk away from any disaster!

These Australasian gannets are extreme survivors at sea.

The sea can be extremely dangerous, especially if you're a gannet. The Australasian gannet is a hunter of fish. So it has a problem. How do you catch a fish when you're soaring 100 feet above the sea? The solution is simple—if a little extreme.

The gannet is number eight in the countdown because no ordinary animal could survive hitting the sea at 90 miles per hour. Hitting anything at that speed is usually fatal!

With built-in airbags, this gannet thinks nothing of plummeting head-first into the ocean.

But gannets are extreme survivors thanks to their clever design. To make sure they don't swallow water, gannets have no nostril holes and can keep that beak tightly shut upon impact. And their bodies have built-in air bags just under the skin. Right before it dives, a gannet inflates these air pockets to absorb the shock of impact.

Unlike those of gannets, the human body is not built for extreme impacts. So why would anyone make a career of diving into the water at 60 miles an hour?

Welcome to the extreme sport of professional cliff diving. These guys jump from more than twice the height of an Olympic high diver, and they hit the water 9 times harder! One of these human gannets is Dustin Webster. He explains:

> *Why would I jump off of something? Well, unlike some animals it's not for survival, that's for sure. The main reason I like to jump off is for adrenaline. When you first look over the edge, it's a long way down. You can't imagine how far down it is. The height I was going from today is about 63 feet – that's about 19 meters. Pretty high – when you consider the human body's not made for that kind of impact.*

No airbags here! Cliff diver Dustin Webster knows the water can make a pretzel out of him.

The only thing I can tell you is when you hit—you better not relax until you take your first breath of air. Because if you relax, that water's going to tear you apart. It's going to shape you into a pretzel. You'd have to get into a car crash to feel a similar feeling.

When you're in the air, you don't have time to think, "Oh, I'm scared," or anything. It's business at that point. You had better be paying attention or otherwise you're going to get hurt. Cliff diving is really a mental game.

It may be fun, but cliff diving is also extremely dangerous—even when going feet first. That's why it's best left to those animals with built-in safety equipment.

7 The **Guanaco**

Our next tough customer lives high in the Andes of South America. It's a cousin of the camel, but it survives extreme height instead of extreme heat. Meet the guanaco.

Needing only one-third of the oxygen as humans, the guanaco can survive at extreme altitudes.

The guanaco can be found more than 3 miles above sea level. Up here the air is dangerously thin. It contains only a third of the oxygen it would at sea level. That's why the guanaco is number seven in our countdown. It's perfectly adapted for living in conditions that would leave us gasping for breath.

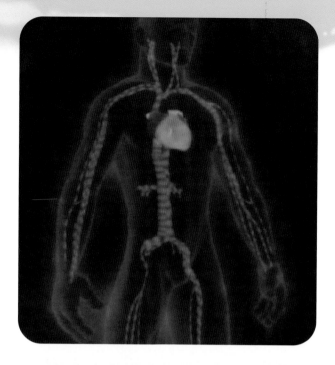

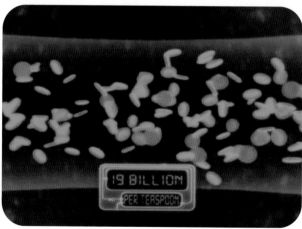

Nineteen billion red blood cells per teaspoon of human blood carry oxygen to the heart.

Imagine if you were dropped onto a mountain 11,000 feet above sea level. At this elevation you'd soon be feeling sick and tired because the organs of your body need oxygen to work properly. And oxygen is carried by red blood cells. In a teaspoon of blood, there are about 19 billion of them, which sounds like a lot. But in thin air, it's not enough.

That's why climbing mountains can be a dangerous business. Above 16,000 feet, you're breathing 4 times faster than normal and still not getting enough oxygen. In the death zone above 25,000 feet, your digestive system gives up and, in a desperate search for oxygen, starts to eat itself. It's not a nice way to go. But imagine if humans were like the guanaco.

A human with guanaco blood would have four times as many red blood cells, and each blood cell would live twice as long. With so many more cells to collect oxygen from the thin air, the guanaco is much better suited to the high life than we are.

The guanaco was once described as "a careless mixture of parts intended for other beasts and turned down as below standard." But like all our other contenders in our countdown, when it comes to extreme survival, this "careless mixture" can teach us a thing or two!

She may not be a zoo favorite, but this guanaco can scale higher mountains than humans.

6

The **Cockroach**

If rats are our worst nightmare, then cockroaches must be what rats have bad dreams about. These belligerent bugs are number six in our countdown because they'll survive just about anything we throw at them.

With a second brain in its rear, the cockroach is a real smarty-pants.

And no wonder. Thanks to super-sensitive antennae, and an extra brain in their rear, cockroaches can dodge just about anything! Of course, they've had plenty of practice—some 400 million years of practice, in fact. Cockroaches were bugging dinosaurs long before they set foot in your kitchen!

You can't live for a month without your head, but this guy can!

From the suburban kitchens of Natick, Massachusetts, comes the ultimate cockroach survival story. Thirty years ago, scientists at the local army base were carrying out experiments on giant Madagascan hissing cockroaches. They exposed the bugs to doses of radiation.

Cockroaches can survive 200 times more radiation than we can. So at the end of the experiment, the scientists were left with a colony of radioactive roaches. They decided they'd better poison the bugs, and then seal them in plastic bags to be taken to the local landfill.

But these bugs just didn't know when to quit. They shrugged off the poison, chewed out of the bags, and were soon running amok in the suburbs. That's why the army decreed the only reliable way to kill these bugs was to hit them with a hammer. You'd have to aim carefully, though. Cockroaches can live for a month with no head, and only then die of thirst.

An extreme will to live helped cockroaches in Natick, Massachusetts, survive radiation, poison, and attempted suffocation.

The Tubeworm

To find the fifth contender in our countdown, we're dredging the bottom of the sea. We're looking for an animal so tough it bathes in acid every day and dines on nothing but poisons!

You can't find number five in the countdown with a snorkel. You need Alvin. Alvin is a deep-sea exploration vehicle. The deep sea is just like deep space—dark, dangerous, and unknown. So Alvin has to be built to withstand the most extreme conditions nature can throw at it.

Imagine traveling a mile and a half straight down. Sunlight disappears after only a few hundred feet. You'd think nothing could survive down here. And then out of the barren wastes rises a miniature volcano. It's a chimney called a "black smoker" that spews boiling hot toxic chemicals into the sea. It would take something really tough to survive here. Something as tough as … the tubeworm.

Alvin was designed specifically for exploring the extreme depths of the sea.

Tubeworms are very strange animals. They're full of billions of bacteria that convert the black smoker's toxic chemicals into food for the worm. That's why the tubeworm has no mouth, no stomach, and no rear end! Yet it survives horrific conditions that would kill any other animal!

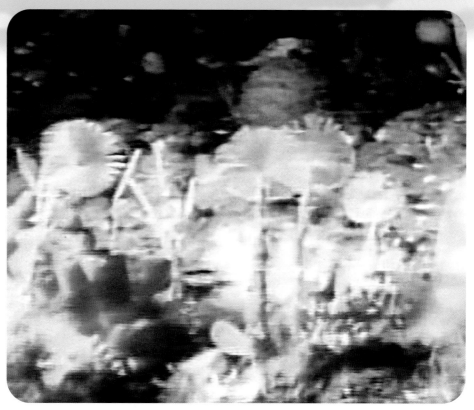

Acidic waters, boiling temperatures, intense water pressure—tubeworm paradise.

Imagine if you were as tough as a tubeworm. You'd spend your life sitting in a bath of vinegar, just like the acid waters of the black smoker. And you'd be breathing hydrogen sulphide—a gas as deadly as cyanide.

Your feet would be in water just above freezing, but your head would be cooking in wafts of boiling water coming from the vent. But the most deadly of all is the extreme pressure of all that water above you. It's like trying to breathe with a blue whale on your chest—pushing down at more than 3,000 pounds per square inch!

We may not be able to survive 2 miles under the surface, but Tanya Streeter from the Cayman Islands gives it her best shot! Tanya is a free diver. That means she takes one big breath, and finds out how low she can go.

Can you imagine holding your breath for two and a half minutes? And once you pass 200 feet, your lungs will be squeezed to the size of eggcups as the pressure collapses your chest cavity!

But going down is the easy part. On her deepest dives, Tanya has to swim the height of the Statue of Liberty to get back to the surface! And all this on a single breath!

Tanya Streeter takes snorkeling to the extreme. But even Tanya would have to dive 20 times deeper to visit the realm of the tubeworm.

Free diver Tanya Streeter is good at what she does, but tubeworm depths would kill her.

The **Polar Bear**

When nature calls, our next contender has learned to hold out even longer than Tanya. Welcome to the Arctic. In this frozen world, animals have to find ways to survive extreme cold. Coming in at number four are the biggest survivors on our extreme countdown . . . polar bears.

Two coats of fur dress these polar bears for success in the freezing Arctic.

An average polar bear has a 5-inch layer of fat and two coats of fur to keep it warm. In fact, an adult bear will suffer more from overheating in the summer than being cold in winter. But baby bears are not so well insulated. That's why pregnant females have to find another way to escape the worst of the Arctic weather. So they go underground.

Deep inside this snow cave a female polar bear will tuck herself away from the worst of the Arctic winter. She'll spend 4 months in this den, saving energy by falling into a deep, deep sleep.

The bear's heart rate will drop to 8 beats a minute and her metabolism will slow to half its normal rate. And she'll give birth to her cubs in her sleep. But the reason the polar bear is number four in the countdown is that during the entire 4 months she's asleep, she won't go to the bathroom. Not once. Not only is that extreme willpower—it's extremely interesting to scientists.

That's because scientists believe the polar bear's ability to grin and "bear it" may help sick humans as well. It's just a matter of hunting down the secrets of the bear's metabolism.

When this polar bear hibernates, she'll be out for the count.

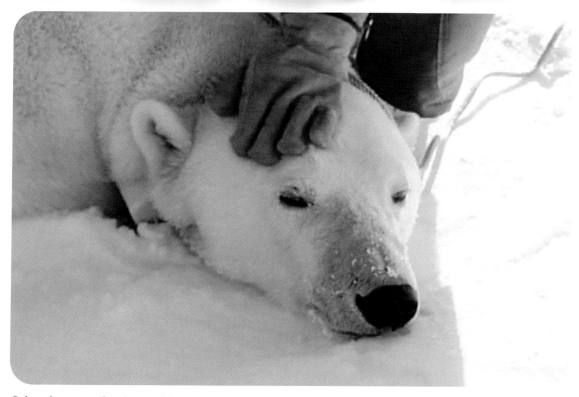

Scientists are fascinated by polar bears' ability to "hold it" all winter.

Scientists are taking a closer look at tranquilized bears because they're the ultimate recyclers. Instead of going to the toilet, hibernating bears turn wastes into protein! Somehow bears are able to split up the waste molecules and use the components to build helpful chemicals that can be used by their bodies.

Scientists are hoping that by analyzing the bears' chemical recycling process, we could develop drugs for people with kidney failure. Patients could recycle their wastes rather than rely on dialysis machines to filter their blood for them.

3

The Emperor
Penguin

It seems incredible that anything could be tougher than polar bears, tubeworms, and cockroaches. But number three in our countdown is an animal that makes the coldest place on earth seem like a tropical paradise!

Need a place to hatch your young? Follow these emperor penguins to Antarctica, the coldest place on earth.

In Antarctica, cold is taken to the most extreme. In some places the average temperature is -72 degrees, and can get down to a world record -129 degrees Fahrenheit.

Few humans would think of spending the winter in Antarctica. After all, in these temperatures, exposed skin freezes in less than a minute. Yet number three in our countdown walks here in bare feet!

These are emperor penguins. At the beginning of the winter, when the sea freezes over and the going gets tough, most animals head north for warmer places. But not the emperors. These incredible survivors choose to breed in the coldest place on earth. They waddle and slide up to 50 miles to reach their breeding ground, where they huddle together to keep out the worst of the wind.

Come freezing temperatures, winds, and snowstorms, papa penguin sees the newly laid egg through the winter.

The females each lay a single egg and then they leave the males to it! The colony of solo dads is plunged into the perpetual darkness of the Antarctic winter.

The males have a problem, though. There's nothing to build nests out of in this frozen wilderness. So they make a nest of their feet. They balance the precious egg on top of their toes and cover it with a warm pouch of skin. And then they settle down for the winter.

They barely move for 65 days. They keep that egg on their toes despite freezing temperatures, cruel winds, and blinding storms. And throughout it all they don't eat a mouthful of food. When the sun finally returns, it's a huge relief for everyone who spent the winter on the ice.

Sometimes, humans in the Antarctic try to compete with the penguins. The arrival of the spring signals the annual Scott Base polar plunge. The rules are simple—no clothes allowed, and you must go completely under. It's got to be a quick dip because cold water robs body heat 32 times faster than cold air. In freezing waters it only takes minutes to stop your heart.

In March 1975, an 18-year-old Michigan man was out for a walk when he fell through the ice. He was submerged in freezing water for 38 minutes. When rescuers pulled his body from the water there were no signs of life.

He was on his way to the morgue, when suddenly he came back to life. He had survived thanks to the mammalian diving reflex. This shuts down all the body systems except those necessary to keep the heart and brain alive. In extremely cold water, it can keep humans (and other more expert divers) alive for a long time.

Submerged emperor penguins are also thought to be able to reduce blood flow to all but the most vital organs. That's why they can spend almost 20 minutes underwater on a single breath!

Adapted to survive extremely cold water, emperor penguins can remain submerged for nearly 20 minutes.

Once back on the ice, the female emperors head back to their hungry males. It's a good thing the females spent the winter feeding, because now the eggs have hatched and there's an extra mouth to feed.

To survive in this frozen world, you have to be tough. Emperor chicks need to keep on their toes. If they fell onto the ice they could freeze to death in only 2 minutes.

The **Weta**

In the mountains of New Zealand, number two in our countdown has a truly extreme solution to surviving the cold winter. It's a huge flightless cricket called a weta.

Weta-sicle, anyone?
When the temperature drops,
this cricket's insides turn to ice.

This tough insect has an armor-plated body and massive
jaws. But unlike polar bears or penguins, it's cold-blooded.
So when the temperature drops, the weta chills out.

The weta freezes solid. Its heart stops beating and all
brain function ceases as the water in its body turns
to ice—sometimes for several months.

**In the spring, the weta defrosts
and carries on good as new.**

It takes a very special kind of animal to survive these freezing conditions. Even experts can only survive for a few minutes. Unlike the weta, we're in big trouble if ice crystals start forming in our cells. Ice crystals are big, sharp, and destructive. When mountaineers have ice crystals forming in their body, its called frostbite.

Ice destroys every cell it touches because it ruptures delicate cell membranes. Even when the frostbitten areas warm up and the ice melts, all the cells are dead and destroyed. And that can lead to gangrene, and amputation.

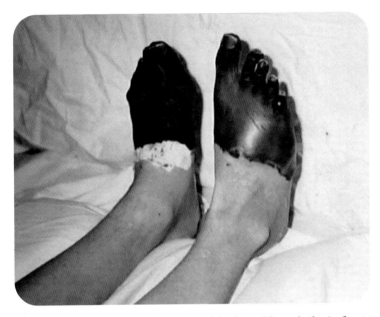

The black dead-cell areas on this frostbite victim's feet will probably need amputation.

But not for the weta. For when the thaw begins, the weta comes back from the dead. There's no frostbite. There's no cell damage. The weta's just been in suspended animation. And scientists still have no idea how it survives. But even the weta's incredible endurance is still no match for the ultimate survivor on the planet.

1

The **Water Bear**

Our number one most extreme survivor is so tough you can find it just about anywhere on the planet—from the bottom of the ocean to the top of the Himalayas.

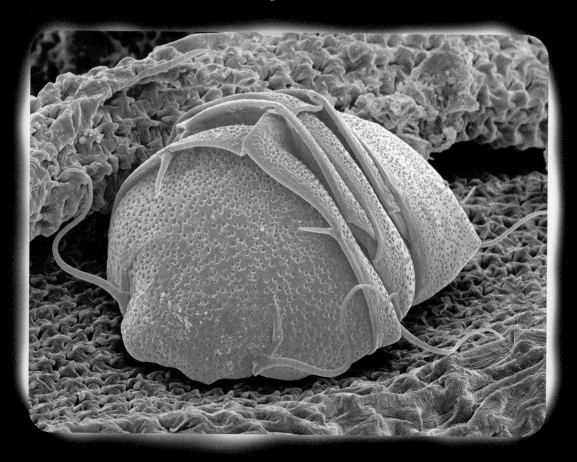

It can survive in hot springs and freezing Arctic wastelands, dry deserts and humid rain forests.

And it can even survive in your backyard. You can find the most extreme survivor anywhere there's moss or lichen. The only problem is that the world's toughest animal is very, very small—invisible to the naked eye, in fact. Coming in at number one in the countdown is the water bear.

A moss-sucking survivor, the water bear is too small to be detected by the naked eye.

Normally this tiny animal waddles around on its four pairs of plump little legs sucking the juices out of mosses and lichens. But when the going gets tough, the cute and squishy water bear can be tougher than a grizzly bear!

The water bear is the most extreme survivor on the planet because when conditions get tough, this animal effectively curls up and dies. It loses 99 percent of the water in its body and enters a state of suspended animation. It will shrink, retract all its legs, and shut down all systems until

On a bad day the water bear
can just shut itself off.

-328°
FAHRENHEIT

At -328 degrees Fahrenheit as human would hope to just curl up and die—and probably would.

conditions improve. Once a water bear is in this state, it's practically indestructible. Water bears can survive temperatures as low as -328 degrees Fahrenheit! Nor is extreme heat a problem. Water bears have survived a scorching 303 degrees!

Imagine if a human was exposed to radioactive material. You could be 150 miles downwind from a nuclear blast and still get a lethal dose of fallout.

The mighty water bear can survive 1,000 times a lethal dose of radiation.

That's about 500 roentgens—the units used to measure radiation. The indestructible water bear has been shown to survive 1,000 times that amount!

Life in the desert would be no trouble for a water bear, either. With nothing to drink, most humans would last less than 2 days. But even camels are no match for one incredible water bear. A long time ago a water bear was trapped in a museum specimen of dried moss. It came back to life when scientists added water to the moss—120 years later! It seems you can never judge an animal by its soft and squishy looks. After all, when it comes to survival, the water bear really is The Most Extreme.

With a little water, a water bear like this one once came back to life after an extreme 120-year hibernation.

For More Information

Richard Conniff, *Rats! The Good, the Bad, and the Ugly.* New York: Crown, 2002.

Eleanor J. Hall, *Polar Bears.* San Diego: KidHaven, 2001.

Liza Jacobs, *Cockroaches.* San Diego: Blackbirch, 2003.

Sandra Markle, *Outside and Inside Rats and Mice.* New York: Simon and Schuster, 2001.

Sandra Markle, *Polar Bears.* Minneapolis, MN: Lerner, 2004.

Patrick Merrick, *Cockroaches.* Chanhassen, MN: Child's World, 2003.

Julie Murray, *Polar Bears.* Edina, MN: ABDO, 2004.

Jason and Judy Stone, *Polar Bear.* San Diego: Blackbirch, 2001.

Erin Pembrey Swan, *Penguins: From Emperors to Macaronis.* Danbury, CT: Scholastic, 2003.

Patricia Whitehouse, *Rats.* Chicago: Heinemann, 2002.

Glossary

adrenaline: a hormone that helps the body deal with stress

arid: extremely dry

cholesterol: a substance found in animal tissues; a high level in the bloodstream is linked with heart disease

cyanide: an extremely poisonous salt

digestive system: the system in the body that breaks down food

fallout: radioactive particles released after a nuclear explosion

gangrene: the death of soft tissues in the body, resulting from lack of blood flow

gastritis: inflammation of the stomach lining

immunity: resistance to a particular disease or substance

lichen: plants that consist of both algae and fungi

mammalian: characteristic of mammals

metabolism: all the chemical processes in a living organism

molecule: tiny particle of matter

prolific: fertile

toxic: poisonous

volatile: evaporating easily

Index